To Robert & Jennifer

I would like to gratefully acknowledge the kind contributions made by the following in the production of this book:

Lorraine White; for bringing Nelson and his friends to life in her superb illustrations.

Albany Graphics (John & Trevor); for undertaking all the reprographic work with such enthusiasm and dedication.

Adsetters; for producing such creative typesetting, and pandering to my designer's whims.

Carol; my wife, for all the hard work in typing, telephoning, organising and supporting this project.

Thank you all. In a world that needs a few more 'extraordinary heroes' I have been very lucky to find so many!

Ian Ralph

Grafton Books
A Division of Collins Publishing Group
8 Grafton Street, London W1X 3LA

Published by Grafton Books 1986

British Library Cataloguing in Publication Data

Ralph, Ian
Nelson the mouse.
I. Title
823'.914[J]   PZ7
ISBN 0-246-12996-4

Made and printed in Great Britain by
William Collins Sons & Co Ltd, Glasgow

·NELSON·

THE EXTRAORDINARY ADVENTURES OF A VERY ENGLISH MOUSE

WRITTEN AND DESIGNED
~ BY IAN RALPH ~

ILLUSTRATED BY LORRAINE WHITE

FOREWORD BY
H.R.H. THE PRINCESS ANNE

FOREWORD

BUCKINGHAM PALACE

  The story of how Nelson the mouse became the village hero has already received critical acclaim - first from author Ian Ralph's own children and then from pupils at the local school. Encouraged by Nelson's success with this most demanding audience, Mr. Ralph decided to seek a publisher for the story, which had originally been written to entertain his family. His aim was to raise money for the members of Save the Children's worldwide family and he is generously donating his royalties to the Fund.

  I would like to thank Mr. Ralph for his persistence and Grafton Books for their perspicacity in bringing the acquaintance of Nelson to a much wider public and much needed funds for children all over the world.

Anne

CHAPTER ONE

he little families of mice that live behind the grocery shop at Tumble-on-the-Marsh are a happy community. But that was not always so. Not so long ago the mice had a problem. Well, not so much a problem, more an annoyance – Nelson, self-appointed hero of Tumble-on-the-Marsh. He was always boasting about his great exploits, his adventures in the land across the marsh, his fights with cats and weasels (he even went so far as to wear an Admiral's hat with a large letter N on the front just to impress the other mice). But no-one really believed his tales.

Matters came to a head one wintry evening after the mouse children had been put to bed. All the grown up mice were sitting around the fire in the corner of the yard where Mr Brown, the shopkeeper, had been burning some rubbish. As usual, Nelson was talking about one of his adventures. This time it was the Cricket Match story, when he had sat between the stumps on the cricket field during the tea interval.

ector, a practical sort of mouse, who happened to be the only one who was listening to this story asked,

"What did you do it for?"

As usual, Nelson chose to ignore any questions and carried on telling everybody how much he had frightened the vicar when he came out to bat. When he realised his story was not keeping the mice amused, he tried another one.

"I remember the time when I swam across the duck pond in full view of all the ducks. That was quite a day! It's a good twenty yards and I . . ."

Hector interrupted again,

"Look, Nelson, it's all very well your showing off about your exploits but . . ."

"Showing off!" Nelson's whiskers were bristling with indignation.

"Yes, showing off," Hector continued. "You're just a plain show-off. No-one here has ever seen you on one of your great adventures!"

"Of course you haven't. It's much too dangerous for any of you to be there when I'm being brave."

All the shouting had attracted the attention of the other mice in the group and a scholarly mouse called Bertrand thought it was time to call a halt to the bickering.

Now, now, you two. Stop all this or you will wake the children."

"But it's true," insisted Hector. "We have NEVER seen Nelson do ANY of the deeds he keeps telling us about."

"Well, I must admit I have never seen any of them, either," agreed Bertrand.

"I've told you why," Nelson said trying to stop these questions.

"I've got a good idea," came a little voice from the back of the group. All heads turned. It was Louise, Hector's wife.

"Next time Nelson feels brave and decides to do something to prove it, we can all come and watch . . . from a distance," she said.

"That suits me," said Nelson with all the bravado he could muster.

The trouble was that not one of his stories was really true. Yes, he had sat on the cricket pitch all through the tea interval. But only because he had rested to regain his breath after walking across the field. When the vicar came out to bat after the tea interval Nelson had run for his life, thinking the bat was a weapon to hit him with.

And his swim across the duck pond? The baby ducks had chased him into the pond and he had to swim right across the water to get away from them. All his adventures were a result of his own stupidity and all his stories of bravery were just a cover-up.

But now, all the mice were nodding in agreement with Louise and mumbling things like "Good idea," or "That will put a stop to his stories."

Suddenly Nelson found himself saying,

"You suggest something – anything – and I'll do it." What was he saying!

Before he could get out of it, Hector cried out,

"Climb the church tower."

"But . . ." Nelson's mind fought for an excuse.

"At night," added Hector doing his best to think of an impossible deed.

To everyone's surprise, including Nelson's, he replied,

"All right, tomorrow night."

Everyone was stunned; so Nelson was going to do it! Hector felt very ashamed. He had not for a moment thought Nelson would do it. Nor had Nelson! But it was too late and nothing the other mice said could make him change his mind because if there was one thing Nelson had it was pride.

That night all the mice went to bed quietly and solemnly.

CHAPTER TWO

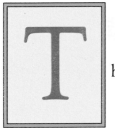

The next morning, the day of the Great Climb, Nelson woke feeling very nervous. A sleepless night spent worrying had made one thing clear – if he could climb the tower and return, he would be a hero forever.

The morning was spent preparing for his climb. He enlisted the help of all the other mice to collect things he needed. They all seemed more friendly although some of the lady mice looked worried as they passed him on their journeys round the yard.

By early evening all he needed had been collected and he started to prepare his equipment. The mice sat round attentively as he assembled his tools and explained what each one would be used for. He did not know exactly but he chatted away very knowledgeably about crampons and ropes and all the mice seemed to believe every word.

He made a thick belt from a rubber band and tied it round his waist. Into it he pushed a bunch of long pins. On the left side he fitted a pick (made from a match stick with a pin pushed half way through). With the help of the mouse children he twisted five strands of cotton together to make a strong rope. This he looped over his head and under his arm, so the coil hung diagonally across his chest. Hector, still feeling rather ashamed, lent him his best walking boots. It was the least he could do for the doomed hero. Louise stepped forward and wrapped her best winter scarf round his neck.

hen Nelson was ready all the mice marched off across the yard with Nelson in his mountaineering gear leading the way. It was a full moon that night and only a few dark clouds chased across the otherwise starry sky.

Until they reached the imposing iron gates that led to the church, Nelson was the picture of confidence, but he slowed when he came in sight of the dark village church silhouetted against the navy-coloured sky. Hopeful glances flashed from face to face; perhaps he would change his mind? But Nelson had noticed these looks and he quickened his pace.

The mice slipped through the railings and scampered along the gravel path to the church. The night was warm, but most of the mice shivered as they strained their necks to gaze up at the massive tower which seemed to almost touch the moon. The clouds skimming past seemed to make the top of the tower look as though it was moving across the sky and seeing this strange effect, Nelson felt his heart racing even faster than it had before. But it was now or never!

CHAPTER THREE

he mice settled down in the long grass to watch the great event. Nelson was standing at the bottom of the tower and, taking a deep breath, started to climb. The lower part of the tower was covered with ivy and for the first few yards the going was easy. He ran up the thick, dry stems until his legs began to ache and his chest hurt.

"Time for a rest," he thought to himself and settled down under a large polished leaf close to the rough stone of the building. He looked down and gulped. It was a long way down but he was pleased to see the little white and grey shapes in the grass waving at him.

The ivy leaf above him suddenly dipped making him jump. What had caused the sudden movement? Very slowly the leaf moved back to its original position and as it did so a large drop of water rolled off the edge. It was raining.

He saw the mice running in all directions to avoid getting soaked. Looking up he saw a large rain cloud cover the moon. Luckily, the shower passed quickly and seeing his friends once more in position he decided to continue the climb.

But although the rain had stopped, the shiny ivy leaves were now very slippery and the stems holding them were also soaked with water. A couple of times he slipped and just managed to cling on with his aching hands. Each time he slipped the mice on the ground shrieked and covered their eyes.

The trails of ivy were thinning out and Nelson had to push his pins into cracks in the stones to make footholds. He tied the rope round his waist and then around each pin as he climbed up. Every step made him more tired and more afraid. Why had he been so boastful – he should have kept quiet!

His thoughts were interrupted by a terrible sound. From somewhere above his head came a deafening sound of clunking and whirring. The noise was terrible but he managed to hang on. Oh no! The church clock was about to strike. It had not occurred to Nelson when he was planning his climb that the huge round clock high up on all four sides of the tower might strike while he was climbing. The whirring stopped and Nelson forced himself to look up to see if he could work out from this angle just how many times the big bell would strike. Just as he did so a sound louder than he had ever heard shook the tower. D-o-n-g! The vibration made his teeth chatter in his head and powdered stone showered down on his head from the old stones decaying away high above him. He braced himself ready for the next strike but to his relief it never came. Looking up again he saw the thick tip of the minute hand was pointed directly at him so it was half past something. That meant he was safe for the next half an hour. He must hurry!

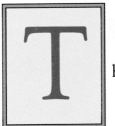he mice on the ground were watching and waiting for the safe return of their friend whom they could barely see. Hector was there with his wife, Louise, and their son, Edward, who was not very bright. He was chasing bits of dried grass on the gravel path near the church door.

Near the church a line of trees stood tall and still against the night sky. At the very top of the tallest tree an owl sat watching little Edward romping around on the gravel. Bright owl-eyes blinked very slowly and long muscular wings spread out as the bird pushed off his branch and circled round behind the tower and hovered above the roof of the church.

Nelson was now struggling to find footholds. He had run out of pins and although his rope was still attached to the highest pin he had to use his little home-made pick to haul himself onto any available ledges. It was now obvious that even if he had brought more pins it would not have been possible to get to the top of the tower – it was much too high.

As he struck a likely looking crack with his pick, Nelson saw the owl. Luckily, it had not seen him but he followed the line of the owl's gaze. Nelson gasped when he saw the tiny dot of white which was Edward still gaily jumping and dancing about far below. Without thinking he pulled the pick out of the wall and flung it with all his might in the direction of the hovering scavenger. As he did so he lost his foothold and fell down, down, down, past rushing stones and ivy until he jerked to a sudden stop as the rope reached its full length. The stop was so sudden that all the breath was squeezed from his body in a shrill scream.

The owl had not been hit by the tiny implement. He had not noticed it but he had heard the squeal as Nelson fell and now he circled round towards this closer, larger mouse. But, as he flew towards the little morsel swinging from the rope a sharp pointed metal stick came flying towards him. Then another and another. Nelson was pulling out the pins below him and was throwing them as hard and as fast as he could at the feathered monster.

By this time the mice on the ground who could see what was happening were jumping up and down, cheering their hero on.

The battle went on with Nelson throwing pins for all he was worth and the owl trying to dodge the steel spikes and lashing out with his sharp claws, trying to capture this crazy little creature. Fortunately he gave up the fight just as Nelson ran out of pins, the only one left was the one holding his rope. He had been climbing up the pins pulling them out as he climbed and now he was at the top of this safety line. The disgruntled owl returned to his lair.

"There will be easier prey than this!" he thought, his pride hurt. Brave, tired Nelson had had enough heroics for one night and swinging hard each way he grasped the welcome ivy and, after untying his safety rope, he clambered slowly but surely down the ladder of stems until he reached the ground – exhausted. A few moments later the big clock struck ten o'clock but Nelson didn't hear it. He was fast asleep!

The next day he awoke to the congratulations of the crowd of smiling mice assembled beside his bed. After a good breakfast little Edward thanked him for saving his life.

Nelson was so happy to be alive he had not even noticed he had lost his Admiral's hat.

And now, if you look in the yard behind the shop, Nelson can be seen listening to the other mice. Some of the mice talk about his Great Climb but he never mentions it – he doesn't have to, does he?

The End